BÀ-NĂM

Written and Illustrated by
JEANNE M. LEE

Henry Holt and Company • New York

Author's Note

This story is based on my childhood experiences in South Vietnam. In Vietnam there is a special day in the year reserved for honoring your ancestors. The day is called Thanh-Minh (tan-min), meaning "pure and bright." On Thanh-Minh Day, families visit the graves of their ancestors and present them with offerings.

I can still remember the trips my family would make to visit my grandfather's grave. The graveyard was on a small parcel of land south of Saigon, the old capital of South Vietnam. We would all squeeze into our old car and when we got there my brothers and I always had a great time, picking fruit and climbing trees.

It was on these trips that I came to know the graveskeeper, an old woman we called Bà-Năm.

It was Thanh-Minh Day and for the first time Nan would be going with her family and relatives to visit the graves of her ancestors.

Nan and her cousin Keung helped her grandmother pack the trunk of their car with incense, flowers, and cakes.

"What is all this for?" Nan asked her grandmother.

"These are offerings for the spirits of our ancestors."

"You'll like going to the graveyard," said Keung. "We can climb trees and pick fruit and we might even see some monkeys."

When they finally arrived at the graveyard, a strange woman was waving to them.

"There's Bà-Năm," said her grandmother. "She is the keeper of our ancestors' graves."

Bà-Năm was standing in front of a small shack and as they got out of the car, Nan noticed that the woman's body was twisted and bent. Her face was covered with deep wrinkles and when she grinned, Nan could see that her teeth were black.

Nan was afraid. She clutched her father's hand and shrank back when the graveskeeper patted her on the head.

After the car was unloaded, everyone walked along a path toward the graveyard.

Soon they came to the graves, which looked like tiny stone houses. Everyone cleaned away the leaves and branches and when they were finished, grandmother and Bà-Năm arranged the offerings in front of each tombstone.

"Come and help us, Nan," said her grandmother.

Nan went to each grave, putting three sticks of incense in each ash container. Then she kneeled down next to Keung to pray, while her grandmother burned paper money.

"Why are you burning money?" asked Nan.

"To send it to our ancestors in the spirit world," her grandmother replied softly.

"Let's go climb trees," Keung whispered in Nan's ear. Nan was glad to get away from Bà-Năm's scary presence.

Keung led her into the woods and Nan looked around her in amazement. She had never seen so many different types of fruit trees.

They picked some juicy fruit from the lowest branches and sat down to eat. Through the trees, Nan could see Bà-Năm gathering more fruit for the graves.

"Why does Bà-Năm have black teeth?" she asked Keung.

"She stained them black to stop decay," he replied.

"She frightens me," Nan said softly.

"She's just an old woman," said Keung, getting up on his feet. He started to run deeper into the woods, leaving Nan alone.

"Wait for me!" she cried.

By the time she caught up with Keung, he had climbed up a tree.

"Catch!" he said, throwing her a big yellow fruit. "It's a papaya."

Nan felt a wet breeze against her face. The sun disappeared behind the clouds.

"Maybe we should go back to the others," said Nan, looking at the sky.

"But I haven't climbed the mango trees," Keung protested.

Nan loved the sweet taste of mangoes. As she turned to follow her cousin, she thought she heard the sound of thunder.

By the time they reached the grove of mangoes, the sky had turned dark. Keung easily climbed up a tall mango tree. As he dropped the mangoes down to Nan, she felt cool raindrops on her cheeks.

Suddenly, there was a frenzied shriek above Nan's head.

"Monkeys!" she yelled. "Get down!"

Keung quickly slid down the tree and the monkeys did not follow. A big gust of wind made the branches of the trees sway back and forth. There was a sudden crack of thunder, which made the monkeys shriek louder.

"Monkeys do not like thunder," said Keung.

They ran through the rain until they came to a line of bamboo.

"This is the wrong way," sighed Keung. "Bamboo marks the edge of the graveyard."

They retraced their steps and took another trail. The rain was falling heavily now and they could barely see through the darkness. The woods were filled with the sound of creaking trees and there were strange shapes everywhere.

Nan was afraid.

Suddenly, there was a new sound above their heads.

"Bats!" cried Keung.

They dropped down and covered their heads with their hands as hundreds of bats flew above them. Nan began to cry. Keung put his arm around her and pulled her close.

"Don't worry," whispered a voice in the darkness. "They won't hurt you."

"Bà-Năm!" exclaimed Keung. "Come on, Nan, Bà-Năm will take us back."

Nan didn't move. "I'm afraid of her," she sobbed.

Bà-Năm crouched down and patted Nan on the head. "We don't want a tree to fall on you, do we?" she said softly. "One fell on me one stormy night long ago."

Nan stood up slowly, took Keung's hand, and they followed Bà-Năm as she led them back to her shack.

Through the darkness, Keung could see the shapes of the graves. He stopped walking.

"What's wrong?" asked Bà-Năm. "Are you afraid of ghosts?"

"Yes," he said quietly.

"The spirits of your ancestors will not hurt you," said Bà-Năm. "They are all happy spirits. Come."

Keung reluctantly walked through the graveyard, keeping close to Bà-Năm.

Nan had stopped crying. She was glad Bà-Năm had found them and felt safe with her.

As they came closer to the last grave they saw the light of Bà-Năm's hut in the distance.

Suddenly, lightning struck.

Nan screamed.

Bà-Năm quickly grabbed her and ran to the last grave. There was a loud crack behind them. Just as Bà-Năm pulled Nan down next to the grave, a large tree fell with a deafening crash just a few feet from where they lay.

Keung had disappeared into the darkness. Nan and Bà-Năm were alone, clinging to each other in the rain.

Slowly, they got up and tramped on toward the shack, where Keung and the others waited on the steps.

The next morning the graveyard was littered with fruit, knocked down by the fierce storm. Everyone went outside to gather fruit to take home.

"You don't have to climb trees today, Keung," teased grandmother.

Bà-Năm smiled when Nan brought her an armful of mangoes. They had decided not to tell the family about their encounter with the tree. It would be their secret.

It was time to leave. When Nan stepped into the car she heard her grandmother talking to Bà-Năm.

"Thank you for bringing Nan and Keung home last night," she said. "You are a blessing to our family."

As the car drove away, Nan turned and waved goodbye to her new friend.

To Patrick

Copyright © 1987 by Jeanne M. Lee

All rights reserved including the right to reproduce this book
or portions thereof in any form. Published by Henry Holt
and Company, Inc., 521 Fifth Avenue, New York, New York 10175.
Distributed in Canada by Fitzhenry & Whiteside Limited,
195 Allstate Parkway, Markham, Ontario L3R 4T8.

Library of Congress Cataloging in Publication Data
Lee, Jeanne M.
    Bà-Năm.
    Summary: A young Vietnamese girl visiting the graves
of her ancestors finds the old graveskeeper frightening
until a severe storm reveals the old woman's kindness.
[1. Vietnam—Fiction.   2. Cemeteries—Fiction.
3. Old age—Fiction]   I. Title.
PZ7.L51252Ban   1987   [E]   86-27127

ISBN: 0-8050-0169-7

First Edition

Printed in Italy

10   9   8   7   6   5   4   3   2   1

ISBN 0-8050-0169-7

DATE DUE
